TYNE & WEAR
FOLK TALES
FOR CHILDREN

To Africa Class,

Enjoy the tales!

from Adam Bushnell
2019

TYNE & WEAR

FOLK TALES
FOR CHILDREN

ADAM BUSHNELL AND DAVE SILK

ILLUSTRATED BY NIGEL CLIFTON

The History Press

First published 2018

The History Press
The Mill, Brimscombe Port
Stroud, Gloucestershire, GL5 2QG
www.thehistorypress.co.uk

British Library Cataloguing in Publication Data.
A catalogue record for this book is available from the British Library.

ISBN 978 0 7509 8801 8

Typesetting and origination by The History Press
Printed and bound in Great Britain by TJ International Ltd

CONTENTS

ACKNOWLEDGEMENTS

We would both like to thank The History Press for asking us to write this book. We'd also like to thank Durham Cathedral, Newcastle Castle and Hylton Castle for their continued support to us both.

Enormous thanks to Nigel Clifton, the awesome and talented illustrator of this book.

Adam would also like to express his gratitude to Sarah, Michael, Lorna, Isla and his parents for their patience and support.

Thanks also to Chris Bostock, Paul Martin, Ian McKone; and editors Harry and Dee.

Dave would like to thank his mam and Becky for persuading him to write this (and lending him the laptop). He would also like to thank his fellow Moss Troopers, Jez Hunt and Mica Hind, for being a constant source of useful nonsense, inane chatter and patient friendship, and Pearl Saddington for getting him into this line of business in the first place!

INTRODUCTION

It was a real challenge to select which folk tales from the rivers Tyne and Wear we would tell in this collection for children. There were some monsters that simply had to go into the book, such as The Lambton Worm and the Bishop Auckland boar. There were some characters that needed to be included too, such as St Cuthbert and Jackey Johnson. In the end, we went with a mixture of well-known tales and those not so well known. We also added new characters such as Tia Maria, the wise witch, too.

Even though the book is aimed at children, we want the tales to be enjoyed by anyone who reads them. They can be read alone or be told aloud to an audience. The tone of voice is meant to be that of a local lad sharing the tales of the past with the whole community: tales that have been told many times before across the whole of the North East of England, but perhaps never quite like this.

Hold on to your flat caps and your whippets, ladies and gentlemen. These folk tales are not your ordinary retellings. There are triple-plaited nasal hairs, donkeys that zoom across the sky and witches that don't use broomsticks to fly but plates on their feet! There's more madness and shenanigans within these pages than can be kept in a wizard's cave.

So read on to find something old, something new, something borrowed and it's all just for you!

RUDE RABBIT

The people of Castle Eden Dene were shocked. As shocked as finding a kitten in a carrier bag! That's how shocked they were. And it was all down to a rabbit.

It had begun as something that they thought of as quite funny. At first, anyway. Some little black rabbit had started to watch the villagers as they went about their daily business. It sat and eyed them curiously.

'There he is again!' they would laugh when the furry bundle would sit and watch.

'It's so cute!' laughed a small girl.

'I want it as my pet!' declared her friend.

But then the rabbit began not just to watch but to interfere with the daily business in the village.

When the maids would go to milk the cows, they found that the rabbit had beaten them to it! The milk was already taken. Drunk dry by the little furry fiend.

When the blacksmith was looking for his hammer, the rabbit had hidden it. Actually, taken it and buried it out in the fields!

When the fisherman had gone down to the river, he found his fishing lines had been chewed right through.

'That's it!' bellowed the farmer.

'What's it?' asked his wife.

'That rabbit!'

'What about it?'

'It has to go!'

'Go where?'

The farmer jumped to his feet. 'Right into the jaws of my hunting dog, that's where!'

Soon a bit of a crowd was following the farmer as he huffed and puffed to the edge of the village. He was dragging along a rather dishevelled-looking greyhound named Bolt.

'Right, Bolt.' The farmer grinned. 'You see that rabbit, there?'

Bolt looked into the distance. He didn't reply. He didn't nod. But the farmer knew he understood every word.

'Get him!'

Bolt scratched his ear with his back leg and then sat down.

'Bolt!' the farmer said, stamping his foot. 'Get that rabbit!' The farmer gave Bolt a nudge and he was off chasing after the rabbit. Now you might think that a greyhound racing over the land toward its prey might make a rabbit move. But this rabbit did not. It just sat there with an almost mischievous grin upon its face.

Bolt drew nearer.

The rabbit just sat there.

Bolt was almost on top of the furry creature.

It didn't even blink.

Bolt leapt into the air.

The rabbit stepped to one side and Bolt landed in a gigantic heap of cow poo. Splat!

The rabbit turned and looked at the villagers. It stuck out its tongue and did a long and loud raspberry sound.

THHHHHPPPPPPTTTTTTTTT!

With that, it was off.

The farmer was furious! Bolt wasn't too happy either.

'Don't worry!' called the blacksmith. 'We'll ALL get our dogs and be ready for him tomorrow!'

The very next day, the villagers were ready. No fewer than twelve fine hunting dogs were gathered at the edge of the field where the rabbit always showed up first. There were three greyhounds, two beagles and seven dogs whose breed could have been anything. They were up early and they were ready!

'Here he comes!' snarled the farmer.

Bolt sat upright. He did not like baths yet had to take one yesterday. He growled when he saw the rabbit appear from the hedgerow.

The rabbit stopped when it saw the crowd ready and waiting. Then it turned its tail to them and started waving it at them.

'Is it teasing us?' a boy asked.

'Well it's twerking its tail,' a girl sighed. 'What else do you think its doing?'

Then the rabbit turned to the villagers and gave out another enormous

THHHHHPPPPPPTTTTTTTTT!

That was it. Bolt was off. The other dogs ran close behind. The rabbit continued to do its weird dance, all the while making trump sound after trump sound.

It was only when the dogs were impossibly close that the rabbit turned and zoomed in and out of the hedgerow. The dogs bounded after it and each one got stuck! They whined and whimpered from the thorny hedges. They cried and called for their owners. All the while the rabbit seemed to be laughing! It was enjoying itself. It gave each dog a little kick before disappearing into the hedgerow for one last time.

'What are we going to do?' asked the farmer, once Bolt had been freed from the hedge. 'That rabbit is making us look like fools!'

'We'll go see the only one who knows about these things!' announced the blacksmith. 'We'll go see the wise woman … Tia Maria!'

Everyone nodded and carried their wounded dogs through the village and over to Tia's house. They knocked. They waited.

Eventually the door was flung open and there was Tia Maria in all her glory. She was around 90 years old but didn't look a day over 172. She had one eye that was looking at you and one eye that was looking for you. Her nasal hair was plaited in three parts. She was quite a sight.

'Hiya!' she croaked.

Everyone mumbled a miserable greeting in return.

'What's up?' she enquired.

'It's that rabbit,' the farmer said. 'You must have seen it. Been up to all kinds of mischief!'

'I still haven't found my hammer!' complained the blacksmith.

Tia Maria nodded. 'It is no ordinary rabbit!' she rasped. 'You'll never catch it but you might be able to follow it.'

'How?' asked the farmer. 'It leaves no tracks or trace!'

'It does, but you can't sense it.' She let her words hang there for a few moments. 'You need help from a creature that can follow scents!' she explained.

'What, like a bloodhound?' asked the blacksmith.

She nodded and snapped her fingers. 'You've got it!'

With that, she slammed her door shut and began singing inside her house.

'I've got a mate in Hesleden who has a bloodhound.' The blacksmith grinned. 'I'll go get it and we can wait for the rabbit to come along in the morning!'

A great cheer went up. The people were happy. They knew they could always rely on the wisdom of Tia Maria.

The next morning, the villagers were gathered at the edge of the field once more. The atmosphere was as heavy as dragon dung. And dragons poop stone.

It seemed like seconds were passing as hours but at last the rabbit appeared. It stuck its head out of the hedgerow and revealed its pink tongue again.

THHHHHPPPPPPTTTTTTTTT!

The villagers were off towards the rabbit. It seemed to laugh and jumped into the hedgerow. It zipped and darted in and out. It leapt this way and that.

The blacksmith led the bloodhound angrily on. When the rabbit saw that, it stopped. It seemed to hold an expression of surprise upon its furry face. Then it turned and ran off.

The blacksmith gave a triumphant laugh.

'Ha!' he guffawed. 'That's done it! We'll follow it to its home!'

The rabbit raced into the dene. It ran from tree to tree, and the villagers and the dogs followed its every move, the bloodhound in front as it pulled at the lead, straining to follow the scent of the crazy creature. They spent all day going around and around. Now the rabbit was tiring. It was slower than before.

It was then that the blacksmith let the bloodhound off the lead. It jumped and snapped and caught the rabbit's leg. The rabbit squealed and kicked at the dog's face. The dog let go and the rabbit zoomed off.

'He's lost it!' shouted the farmer.

'He's lost nothing,' grinned the blacksmith. 'We've got it now!'

The lead was now back on the bloodhound. The blacksmith and the villagers were led through the dene and out to the other side. They came to the village of Easington. All the while the bloodhound led them along, pulling and panting as it went.

They walked right to the other side of the village. There they came to a house. The bloodhound barked and scratched at the door.

'In there?' asked the farmer.

'I guess so!' replied the blacksmith.

He opened the door and sitting there by the fire was a woman older than Tia Maria. She was rubbing her leg, which had tooth marks on it. The tooth marks from a bloodhound.

'You're the rabbit?!' asked a shocked blacksmith.

'She's a witch!' screeched the farmer.

'That's right,' the old woman squawked back at them, 'and if you don't get out of here, I'm going to turn you into sausages or bananas or something much worse!'

The villagers screamed and ran off. They never dared to go back to Easington for fear of being turned into something worse than a sausage.

THE WIZARD'S CAVE

You might have visited Tynemouth for the sea air, or to walk your dog on the beach. You might have gone up to the headland and seen the ruins of the great castle and priory there, and maybe walked around the gloomy gravestones while looking out on the wild North Sea, if you enjoy that kind of thing.

But you probably won't have heard tell of the Wizard's Cave. Few people know about it these days, though once upon a time this story was as familiar to everyone who lived near the mouth of the Tyne as the story of the Three Billy Goats Gruff, or Red Riding Hood. That's because the Wizard's Cave is long gone, eroded by the sea and collapsed into ruin and rubble, so if this story gives you any ideas to go hunting for any treasure that the hero might have missed, you'll have to think again. Besides, you wouldn't have wanted to go in there anyway – the cave was sometimes known as Jingling Geordie's Hole, and was haunted by the ghost of a long dead smuggler who didn't like company.

But on with our story of Walter the Knight and the Wizard's Cave. Now Walter was the son of Sir Richard, a brave knight who fought with Earl Percy in the old days of border battles, where the sword and the lance were often seen doing their grisly work in the hands of brave warriors from England and Scotland. It should come as no surprise, then, that Walter was taught from a young age to swing a sword and ride a horse and to fear nothing. His mother used to sit the young boy on her knee and tell him tales of brave deeds, deadly battles and mysterious treasures hidden away beneath the earth by demons and wizards.

'The greatest of all these treasures,' she said, 'lies in a cave beneath the great grey towers of Tynemouth. Where the waves lash the cliffs and hooded monks chant, night and day. Many people have tried to seek out this treasure – brave warriors with sharp swords and stout shields; holy men and women with crosses and prayers; even the saintly prior of the Abbey himself once went in search of the treasure.

But no one ever comes back from the dark mouth of that cave once they enter. They say demons and spirits guard the treasure, and only the bravest of souls can defeat them. Anyone who enters that black cave and fails to defeat the monsters within is doomed to live forever beneath the green waves of the sea.'

As a boy Walter was enchanted by his mother's stories of hidden caves, lost treasures and mysterious spells. As he grew up he thought of the cave constantly, even as he began to take on his responsibilities as a knight, fighting on the borders against Scottish raiders for the great Lord Percy. By the time he was sixteen years old he was a great knight – he could ride faster and fight harder than any young man on the borders, and soon the Scottish raiders learned to fear the black raven feather plume of his helm and the sharp sword in his hand.

But however famous he became for his bravery, he always remembered his mother's story about the caves beneath the abbey and the monsters and treasure inside. 'Only the bravest of souls can defeat them,' she had said. Walter longed to prove that he was the bravest knight in the north, and he knew how he could do it.

One day, he packed his armour and weapons onto his horse, and without even his squire for company, he set off for Tynemouth. When he arrived, the weather was wild – it usually is round there, but this day was particularly bad. A sea fret, a thick icy mist, had blown in off the sea, and shrouded the stones of the Priory in a thick grey blanket that soaked Walter to the skin. He could hear the chanting of the monks very faintly from inside the Church, but the sound was almost drowned out by the wild howling of the east wind blowing from the North Sea. He was cold, wet and shivering, but he was not afraid. Walter put on his armour and buckled his sword to his side, then tied a long rope to a large rock at the top of the cliff face. Then he began his downward climb.

His mother had told him that the entrance to the cave was halfway down the cliff face. He didn't rush, making his way foot by foot, inch by inch down the rope, dangling between the Priory at the top and the rocks on the beach at the bottom. One wrong move and he would have tumbled to the bottom and gone 'splat!' The climb seemed to Walter to take all day – his arms were burning with pain by the time he climbed off the rope and into the dark mouth of the cave in the side of the cliff. When he looked to the sky, it was impossible to tell if it was night or day, because the fog was so thick he could see neither the sun nor the moon.

Walter took a wooden torch from a bag over his shoulder, lit it and drew his sword. With his weapon in one hand and the burning torch in the other, he slowly made his way into the tunnel that led from the cave mouth deep into the earth. The path was slippery with sea water and slime, and the tunnel was as cold as the wind outside, and when the wind blew through the cave it made an eerie wailing noise – or was that the wind?

Walter saw, in the dark distance of the tunnel, lights like bright burning eyes of blue flame, and he began to think that the wailing was the voice of the demons that dwelt in the cave. Perhaps he shivered a little, but he showed no fear, gripped his sword tightly and went on. The cave began to grow wider and wider until Walter found himself standing in a great pillared hall far underneath the earth. Tunnels wound off in every direction – this was not going to be an easy task!

He explored every tunnel beneath the earth and found all kinds of terrifying creatures lurking in every corner of the cavern – he defeated dragons with scales of brass and breath of flame; he smashed skeletons with chattering jaws and sharp swords in their bony fists; he slew slithering serpents; squashed giant spiders; and bonked brutal bogles over the bonce – a bogle, if you don't know, is a type of nasty little goblin that lives in the North East and loves to cause all types of trouble. Best to bonk them on the bonce if you see any.

By the time the sun was beginning to creep over the horizon his sword arm was aching with the effort of all the battles he had fought. But he hadn't let fear get the better of him – however terrifying the creatures that had come against him, brave Walter the Knight had held fast and fought them off. Now at last he passed through a great door and into a vast cavern, bigger than anything he could have imagined being beneath the earth.

Inside, the whole place shone as he cast his torch around, showing piles of gold, silver, emeralds, rubies and diamonds. Jewels as big as his fist lay on big piles of coins. Gold-hilted swords hung from the walls, crossed over shining shields with inlaid pictures of silver. He gasped and stuffed as much as he could into his pockets before he heard the demons, dragons and evil creatures beginning to charge into the chamber after him.

It was a hard fight, he had to hack his way back out of the cave – his sword was blunt and his armour dented. But he'd done it! No doubt Sir Walter became a rich knight from the gold and silver that he carried out of the cave.

No doubt he entertained many people with the tales of his adventures beneath Tynemouth crags. No doubt he became famed as the bravest among all the knights who followed the great Lord Percy. But what of the rest of the gold?

The people of Tynemouth searched for it for many a long year – people used to climb the cliff in search of Walter's Cave. Some say eventually a pirate found it, and lived in there until he died. Then his ghost haunted it – the ghost became known as Jingling Geordie, and the cave as Jingling Geordie's Hole. But no one ever found the gold (or at least, if they did, they didn't tell anyone). Eventually, in the 1800s the cave collapsed, and so I suppose now the gold is buried far beneath the earth, just waiting for another brave, or lucky, soul to find it. Perhaps it could be you?

THE
PIG OF
DOOM

Pollard was bored. Bored, bored, bored. He thought he was going to yawn his head off. He wasn't allowed outside. No one was. All because of a stupid pig.

Some huge pig had attacked people in the street and now the Prince Bishop, who ruled this land, had decided it would be safer for everyone if they stayed inside.

Weeks had gone by. Stupid pig.

Pollard looked out of his window. He couldn't believe his eyes. There, standing right outside of house, was the biggest pig he had ever seen in his life. Its round, barrel belly was covered in thick hair like the bristles on a broom. It had tusks like swords that hung from its dripping, drooling mouth. The snout was like an elephant's trunk. The pig's eyes scanned the street. Then it strolled off toward the forest beyond.

Who did that pig think he was? Swaggering and staggering down the street like he owned it. Where was he off to anyway? Pollard looked up at the darkening sky that matched his own mood. The boy was peering through his window when an idea hit him like a flying cream pie. Boom! The pig was off to his bed! The pig was going to sleep in some pit in the forest. That was it! Pollard rubbed his chin and made a 'hmmm' sound. He was thinking. A plan began to form inside his mind.

Before he had decided if the plan was a good one or not he went down the stairs, through the kitchen and off up the street toward the forest. He had collected the largest knife from the kitchen that he could find. He was off to hunt a pig. But he wasn't daft. The pig was HUGE. So, he was going to kill the pig while it slept. There was a grin on Pollard's face as his heart pounded faster and faster.

The forest looked dark and scary. Branches with claw fingers leaned toward him. He stopped. He had to pull himself together. He had to do this. He had two choices; turn back or go on. Sit in his room or be a hero. Pollard gripped the knife tighter in his hand. He gulped and stepped into the forest. The pig had knocked down bushes and brambles, leaving a pretty obvious clue as to where it had gone. Pollard followed the path of destruction. He heard the pig before he saw it. Its noisy snore echoed and bounced off the trees. It sounded like a hippo trying to sing.

Slowly, stealthily and silently, Pollard stepped toward the snoring pig. The barrel belly heaved up and down, up and down. It was hypnotic. Pollard saw the beating heart beneath the thick hairs. He would stab it in the heart and he would be declared a hero. The Prince Bishop might make him a knight or give him money. He might get a lot of money. Pollard smiled at the thought. It would all be worth it. He just needed to kill this pig.

Just then Pollard realized that the snoring had stopped. The pig's eyes were open. Pollard shrieked and jumped out of the pig's pit. The pig snorted. It was louder than a million dragons with megaphones.

The boy began to run but the ground shook under his feet. He turned and saw the pig

charging at him. At the last possible moment, Pollard jumped to one side and landed with a thud on the forest floor. The pig charged past him. Pollard leapt to his feet. The pig snorted in fury. Long, thick drool slopped to the floor with a splat.

The pig scratched the ground in front of it and charged again. Pollard waited until it was almost upon him. Then he jumped to safety again. The pig raged and fumed. It charged again and again. But Pollard was small and fast. Back and forth, back and forth they went. The pig charged and Pollard leapt.

By now, the pig had slowed down. It was exhausted. Its tongue was hanging from its mouth. It sank down to its knees.

This was the moment Pollard needed. He lunged forward with his knife and stabbed the pig in its heart. With a 'blurgh!' it fell down dead.

Pollard sank to his knees. He was exhausted too. He wanted to fall asleep on the forest floor right then and there. But he was worried that someone would come along and steal his precious prize. Pollard rubbed his chin and made a 'hmmm' sound again. Another plan began to form inside his mind. A very unpleasant plan.

He took the pig's long red tongue into his hand. Then, with his other hand, he chopped the tongue out of the pig's mouth. It looked like a long red snake in his hand. Pollard then stuffed the tongue into his pocket and fell fast asleep on the forest floor.

While he slept, a hunter was walking through the forest. He had heard of this killer pig but he had been careful to stay out of its way. Yet, here in front of him was the pig . . . dead! And a boy sleeping beside it. The hunter smiled mischievously.

'There's no way the Prince Bishop will believe that this boy killed that pig,' he whispered gruffly. 'I'll take the pig to the Prince's palace and I'll be rich!'

The hunter silently dragged the pig out of the forest by tying ropes around its back legs. Then he loaded it onto a wagon and was off.

When Pollard woke up, he saw that the pig was gone.

'Someone's nicked me pig!!!' he exclaimed in alarm.

He knew at once what must have happened. He knew at once where to go.

Pollard raced off to the palace of the Prince Bishop in Bishop Auckland. When he got there, he marched straight into the throne room and saw the Prince Bishop counting out golden coins for the hunter. The pig was laid upon the floor for all to see.

'Oi!' shouted Pollard. 'He didn't kill that pig! I did!'

The Prince Bishop looked at the boy and smiled. 'You?' he asked. 'You're only a small boy. How could you have killed this monstrous beast?'

'With this knife!' He held up the blood-stained blade. 'I can prove it too!' he announced.

'How?' asked the Prince Bishop.

'Take a look inside that pig's mouth!' the boy beamed.

The Prince Bishop stood up and nodded to his guards. The mouth was opened and everyone looked inside.

'How come I've got this?' Pollard bellowed and pulled free the red tongue.

He wiggled it around the room. All eyes fell upon the hunter.

'Yeah, erm, well, I'd better be going now.'

The hunter slid from the room. All eyes were now on Pollard.

'Well done young man!' the Prince Bishop said warmly. 'The reward now goes to you, of course.'

Pollard's smile was wide.

'But there's more,' the Prince Bishop went on. 'I'm going to have my lunch now. It's chicken nuggets and chips – it'll be lush. 'Anyway, take a horse from the stable, young man. Ride over the land and back. Whatever land you've ridden over by the time I've eaten my lunch will be yours and yours alone.'

Pollard raced from the room and went straight to the stables.

The Prince Bishop sat down to eat his lunch. But he had only eaten one chicken nugget when Pollard was back.

'That was quick,' the Prince Bishop said, surprised. 'Where have you been?'

'I've been for a ride around your palace. You can move out whenever you like.'

'What?!' spluttered the Prince Bishop.

'You said that any land I've ridden over will be mine and mine alone. Well, I've been around your palace and now its mine. You can move out whenever you like.'

'Right then,' the Prince Bishop replied, surprised. 'I guess I'll be off.'

'I'm only joking!' laughed Pollard. 'The money is enough for me!'

Pollard and the Prince Bishop laughed and laughed. They sat together and ate the nuggets and chips. Pollard's name became famous across the land.

As for the pig? The people of Bishop Auckland ate sausages for a month!

JACKEY JOHNSON

If you had lived in Newcastle in the early part of the 1800s, 180 years ago or thereabouts, you might have thought you lived in a pretty modern, up-and-coming town. George Stephenson had just built the *Rocket* in Newcastle, the most advanced steam engine of the day – engines just like it would soon be pulling trains up and down the length of the country. Richard Grainger was busy planning beautiful new streets and buildings which would see Newcastle transformed from a dark and cramped medieval town into a bright, wealthy and modern place.

But let's say you got ill – sure, you could go to the doctors, but doctors 180 years ago were still happily putting leeches on their patients to suck their blood out, and most of their cures didn't work as they didn't yet know what we know about illness and medicine. Perhaps you might have lost something, or even had something stolen from you – there was no police force yet, so you would have to pay a thief taker to go looking for the person who had stolen from you, and what chance did they have of catching anyone? And maybe, like millions of people who read their star signs in the papers even today, you might have wanted to know what the future held for you, whether you'd get that new job, or who you would marry. If you did, you might have climbed the steep and narrow streets from the Quayside past the ramshackle, half fallen-down houses that loomed over the dark alleys, and gone towards the towering spire of All Saints Church. There, on the street called Dog Bank next to the shops selling furniture and old clothes, stood a large old house with a dark wooden door. You might have shuddered with fear as you knocked on the door, because this was the home of none other than Black Jackey Johnson – the Wizard of Dog Bank!

The newspapers called Jackey (whose real name was John Johnson) a 'professor of the occult science' – but that's just a fancy way of saying Wizard. He was feared and respected by the people of the town. Sometimes, thieves who had stolen things from people would return what they had pinched when they heard that Black Jackey had been hired to find them! People believed he could see the future, find what was lost, turn people invisible and even raise the spirits of the dead, all thanks to his magic book and a deal with the Devil! The story might have gone a little like this …

John Johnson had studied the magic arts for years and years, ever since finding an ancient book of spells in an old bookshop down a dark alley in the depths of the town. It had belonged to the great Wizard Agrippa who had lived hundreds of years ago, and now its secrets had come down to John (or Jackey, as his friends called him). He had practised a great many of the simpler spells: love charms to make a man fall in love with a woman; the charm of 'Abracadabra' which could cure a cold (some of the time); and the Sator Square, which when written on a piece of paper and fed to a cow ensured plenty of milk. But he was hungry for more power, and so one night in May, at the time of the owl-light, he went down to the crossroads outside the town, determined to use his spells to call on the Devil and make a bargain.

As the moon rose, Jackey drew a circle of salt on the ground, then made the signs and said the words in the ancient book – you didn't think I was going to tell you the signs and the words, did you? Oh no, that would be much too dangerous, for this is not the kind of thing you should be meddling with, as you will see…

Jackey waited; and waited; and waited. He waited until the moon disappeared behind the clouds and was just about to turn and go home disappointed, when a fine gentleman dressed all in black and riding on a black horse came galloping across the moor, dismounted and stood in front of him.

'John Johnson, I presume?' said the gentleman and took a book out of a bag which hung at the side of his saddle. Jackey nodded – he didn't need to ask this man's name, for it was obvious enough that he was the Devil.

'Well, be quick. I am a busy man – what is it that you want?' said the gentleman. Then Jackey set out the deal he wanted – he wanted to be given magic powers. Then in seven years' time he wanted the Devil to come back and fill his hat with gold. Then in another six years' time, the Devil could come and claim him, and take him straight to Hell! (I'm afraid this is always the end result of such a deal.)

The Devil seemed fairly pleased with this and took a quill pen from his hat and asked Jackey to sign his name in his great black book – there were a lot of other names signed in there, some in fine handwriting, some scrawled, some so hard to read they looked like a spider had crawled across the page after stepping in ink. Jackey signed and the Devil closed his book and rode off. From then on, Jackey became famous in Newcastle – he had all kinds of strange and amazing powers.

If he boiled a dead cat on a Sunday and then dried it out into a powder, the powder could turn people invisible. He would appear and disappear almost as if he could fly, and there was nothing lost or hidden that Jackey couldn't find. With the money he made selling his special skills, he bought a big old house on Dog Bank and took to dressing all in black so that all the people of Newcastle began to call him Black Jackey Johnson. He lived a life of luxury, at least by the standards of the times (he had no internet to entertain him, so it may not strike you as very luxurious). This went on for seven years, until he was one of the most famous men in Newcastle, even if most people only ever mentioned his name in a whisper.

But after seven years of wild living, his funds were running low. Even though he charged quite a lot for his magical skills, Jackey knew how to have fun, and that usually costs money! So, a few days before the first seven years of his bargain were up, Black Jackey Johnson disappeared from view, and people could hear all kinds of work going on in the house – banging and hammering and digging

and sawing. Then, one dreary day, the Devil knocked on Jackey's door.

Jackey let him in very politely and then showed him into his study and offered him a drink, taking great care to make his guest feel very welcome. In the middle of the floor of the study was Jackey's tall top hat, standing with the top of the hat on the floor and the hole facing up to the ceiling.

'Is this the hat you wish to be filled with gold?' the Devil asked.

'Yes please,' said Jackey. 'Right to the brim!' The Devil clicked his fingers, and in the air above the hat a single gold coin appeared and fell into the hat; then another coin, then another and another and another. Gold kept raining down into Jackey's hat, and it seemed to the Devil as though soon it must be filled – a hat can only hold so many coins after all. But the strange thing was that the hat didn't seem to be getting any fuller at all.

After half an hour of this, the Devil began to tap his feet with impatience. Then he leapt forwards to grab the hat, and as he lifted it up he saw at once that he had been tricked! The top of the hat had been cut away, and the hat had been carefully balanced over a hole in the floor that went straight down into Jackey's brand new basement, which was now filled with gold coins! I don't mind telling you that the Devil was absolutely furious – if he could have turned any redder, he would have. He vanished in a flash and promised that when he returned in six years' time he would dream up something really horrible to do to Jackey in Hell! But Jackey only laughed.

Now six years probably sounds like a long time to you, but when you have the Devil's threats hanging over your head it can feel like it passes in the click of a finger. So it was for Jackey, who worried and fretted as he planned how to get out of his bargain with the Devil.

So it happened that when the Devil arrived on an October night, 13 years since he had first made the bargain with Jackey Johnson on the

Town Moor, he found him doing something that he never expected. Jackey was reading from the Bible.

Now, you might know that as long as a person is busy reading from a holy book, the Devil cannot come near them, and this is true. So it was that Jackey turned his head and said to the Devil, 'I'm nearly ready to come with you, but I am saying my prayers.'

'It's a little late for that Jackey,' said the Devil with an evil grin.

'Nonetheless, I'd like to finish one last prayer – can you give me until this candle burns itself out?'

The Devil looked, and on Jackey's desk was the little stub of a candle – a tiny wee thing that couldn't have more than a minute or two left before it burned out. The Devil laughed. 'Of course. Until that candle burns itself out,' the Devil said.

'Thank you very much,' said Jackey, who licked his thumb and forefinger, grasped the candle wick and, with a 'hiss', put it out himself.

He tucked the stub of the candle into the Bible and closed the book.

The Devil looked eager to get his hands on old Jackey, but Jackey held up his hand to stop him.

'Wait!' Jackey cried out. 'You said I could have until the candle burned ITSELF out. But I have put it out myself and might light it again later. You will have to wait until then, old friend!'

The Devil had been tricked! Again! He raged; he fumed; he swelled up to enormous size and gnashed his teeth; he showed himself in all kinds of horrible scary forms to Jackey, but Jackey only laughed. He had tricked the Devil. The old Bible, with the candle inside, was locked inside a chest in Jackey's basement and never opened again. The Devil vanished back to Hell, and as for Jackey – well, he lived a long and prosperous life, although he was eventually forced to move out of Newcastle and down the river to Byker when the town council got too scared of him. There he lived until, the newspapers tell us, he died at the ripe old age of 71 on 3 April 1837 – Newcastle's last professional Wizard.

JOHNNY REED'S CAT

ohnny Reed was the gravedigger at St Mary's in Staindrop village to the south of the River Wear. He wasn't all that busy as the village wasn't all that big, but he certainly had a busy night ahead of him one cold November.

Old Jim had died and Johnny had to dig the grave for him. Old Jim had been a big man and the grave had to be deep and very wide. Johnny had taken his tools after breakfast and had spent the entire day with his spade for digging and his shovel for scooping. In the morning the ground had been frozen and hard, so he'd had to loosen the soil with a pickaxe. Now it was getting dark and the frost came creeping back. Getting dark and he wasn't even finished! He shook his head.

'You're getting old, Johnny,' he said to himself. 'Old and slow.'

Finally, he was done. In the pitch black of the winter night he put his tools back in the shed round the back of the church house. Then he made his way through the graveyard and back to his own home. He carried a lantern which glowed dimly in the dark. He chuckled at the thought of falling into the fresh grave he had just finished digging.

'That would be a fine pickle to be in!' he said to himself.

Just then, he noticed some lights floating above the ground a little ahead.

'What's this?'

Johnny thought they might be fireflies or glow-worms. He had heard of such things but had never actually seen one himself. He held out the lantern and crept closer.

He saw that there were shadows darker than night itself sitting upon the grass. The glowing lights weren't lights at all but eyes. Glowing green eyes. The shadows were the shapes of cats and there were nine of them altogether. Johnny felt the lantern wobble uncertainly in his hand. Then he heard a voice.

'Johnny Reed!'

'Erm, hello?' Johnny replied, a flicker in his voice. 'Who's there?'

'Johnny Reed! Johnny Reed!' the voice called again.

He swung the lantern back and forth. 'Who's there? Who is it?'

'Johnny Reed! Johnny Reed!'

Johnny stepped forward. All he could see were the cats staring at him, motionless.

'Johnny Reed! Johnny Reed!'

He went to walk around them but they all sat in a line blocking his path.

'Johnny Reed! Johnny Reed!'

The voice was coming from the cats.

'Johnny Reed! Johnny Reed!'

He realised it wasn't one voice. It was nine. All speaking at exactly the same time.

'Johnny Reed! Johnny Reed!'

'Is it you cats that are talking to me?' he asked nervously, the lantern shaking so much he feared the candle inside would go out.

'Yes, it is!' the cats hissed back as one voice.

'Erm, well what do you want with me?'

'Johnny Reed! Johnny Reed!

Tell Madame Momfoot
That Mally Dixon's deed!'

Johnny's face fell. What were these cats talking about?

'Deed?' he asked. 'You mean dead?'

'Howay, man!' the cats called incredulously. 'We're from the North East, ya know! Aye … that's reet …deed!'

'Right, sorry.'

Then the cats called out again:

'Johnny Reed! Johnny Reed!
Tell Madame Momfoot
That Mally Dixon's deed!'

Johnny thought about this. Madame Momfoot? Mally Dixon? He'd never heard of either of them! Then the cats slipped off one by one into the night. Johnny was left holding his lantern, which was a little less shaky now.

He hurried home to his wife and his own pet cat. He wondered what his wife would make of all of this! She was seated by the fire with their little cat curled up on her knee.

'What's wrong with you?' his wife asked.

'You look like you've seen a ghost!'

Johnny told her the whole tale, finishing with the words:

'Johnny Reed! Johnny Reed!

Tell Madame Momfoot

That Mally Dixon's deed!'

His wife looked confused. 'Who's Madame Momfoot? Who's Mally Dixon?'

Johnny shrugged.

Just then, the cat opened her eyes and sat up. She looked at Johnny and his wife. Then, she spoke.

'Mally Dixon's dead, you say?'

Johnny and wife looked on, wide eyed. The cat stretched and jumped off the lap and padded to the door. She looked back at the startled pair.

'I'm Madame Momfoot, even though you know me as Tiddles.'

Johnny and wife opened their mouths to say something but couldn't find the words.

'Mally Dixon dead?' the cat said, shaking her head. 'Who'd have thought?'

Then she nudged the door open with her paw. 'So long, and thanks for all the fish!'

With that, the cat was gone and she was never seen again.

THE
WALLSEND
WITCHES

What does the word 'witch' conjure up in people's imagination? To most people, a witch is nothing more than a Halloween costume – a green face, a pointed nose, a black cat and a broomstick. And yet, there are people who describe themselves as witches to this day, though there is nothing dangerous or frightening about them.

But hundreds of years ago, the word 'witch' made people think of evil people performing evil spells in dark and eerie places – of bargains with the Devil for evil powers, such as the deal that the wizard Black Jackey struck with the Evil One. Many people (mostly, it has to be said, innocent old ladies who had the bad luck to own a cat and a wart and who had upset their neighbours) were executed for the 'crime' of witchcraft.

This story is supposed to have happened in Wallsend – although it's hard to know when it's supposed to have happened, as the first person to tell the story was Sir Francis Blake Delaval, who was famous for exaggerating and making up crazy stories (totally different from the more trustworthy storytellers that you find today…). At any rate, Francis died in 1771, more than 240 years ago, and when he told the story it was already 'once upon a time'. So…

Once upon a time, the lord of Seaton Delaval was riding back to his great hall from a night out in Newcastle (already in these ancient times a place famous for a good night out). His horse was just turning up the road past Wallsend, which was just at the foot of the little hill upon which stood Wallsend Church, when he noticed to his surprise that the inside of the Church was brightly lit, with candlelight streaming through the windows. Now, this was after midnight, when the priest should have been tucked up in his bed, and it didn't seem likely to him that there should be anyone in the Church at this hour. So it was that Lord Delaval decided to investigate.

He left his servant holding his horse at the gates of the churchyard, slowly opened the creaking iron gate, and then walked up past the worn and weathered gravestones scattered throughout the burial ground, until he came to the wall of the Church. He pulled himself up to one of the windows and peered inside to see what he could see. What a sight!

Inside the Church, upon the communion table he saw at each corner a human skull had been placed upside down with a great black candle burning brightly in it, which supplied the light that lit up the whole building and gleamed through the windows. Lying on the table, partially unwrapped from its shroud, was a dead body – Lord Delaval could see a white, limp arm hanging down off the edge of the table. Surrounding the table were four wicked looking hags, like witches straight from a fairy tale – long noses, red eyes and buck teeth, and cackling as loud as you like! One of them held a sharp, gleaming knife in her hand and soon started to chop the fingers from the dead body on the table!

Whether they intended to eat the fingers or use them as ingredients in some horrible

potion, we never learn. At that very moment, angry to see the Church being used in this way, Lord Delaval climbed down from the window, marched straight to the front doors of the Church and charged at them with his shoulders, aiming to break the doors open. With a 'crash' he rushed into the Church and made a grab for one of the witches, knocking over the candles as he went. A rushing wind seemed to fill the Church and buffet Lord Delaval this way and that. All around him he could hear the screams of the witches as they banged and clattered around the old Church in the dark, desperate to escape. He held tight to the ragged cloak of the one witch he had grabbed hold of, and did not let go, no matter how much she squirmed and screeched and scratched at him.

After a long struggle he managed to subdue the witch – I suppose she was old and got tired out quicker than Lord Delaval! He dragged her outside, tied her up and threw her over the back of his horse. Although he was very angry, I suppose he wanted to do things properly and give the witch a fair trial – or as fair a trial as any 'witch' would get in those days!

So, the witch was thrown in jail until the jury and the judges came to Wallsend. It didn't take them very long to find her guilty – after all, she looked just like a witch. She was sentenced to be burned at the stake down on the beach at Seaton Sluice.

On the day of the excecution, a huge crowd of people were gathered down at the beach to watch the burning. A big wooden stake had been hammered into the sand and lots and lots of firewood piled around the base of it. The witch was placed on the pile of firewood and was just about to be tied to the stake when Lord Delaval remembered something. It was considered polite to give a person about to be executed a last request – sometimes people wanted to eat something nice before they died, or to say a few last words to their family.

'Any last requests before we roast you, witch?' cried out Lord Delaval.

'If it would please your lordship,' said the witch, 'I would like two wooden plates that have never been used before, nor washed.'

'Very well,' said Lord Delaval wearily, and the people on the beach all groaned. The burning had to be postponed and they all stood around nervously on the beach, staring at their feet while they waited for a young boy to run back to the village to fetch the two wooden plates the witch had requested. Not one of them seems to have questioned what the witch, who was about to be burned to a cinder, might want with these plates and they didn't stop to ask.

Now let's say you'd been sent running to fetch two plates from a village more than a mile away, and people were waiting for you. You'd run pretty fast, wouldn't you? And if you ran too fast you might trip and fall. Well, that's just what happened to the boy who had been sent to fetch the plates. He tripped and – splash! One of the wooden plates fell into a puddle. Well, he didn't think much of it – you

wouldn't, would you? He just got up, picked it up and kept on running.

Soon, panting and puffing, he got back to the beach and the witch was handed the two plates. She looked very pleased with herself as she placed one plate beneath each foot, mumbled a spell and then, slowly at first then faster and faster, began to rise up into the air! All the people on the beach stared, amazed, then began to cry out and run around pointing their fingers into the sky.

'Look! Look! She's flying away!' they cried out. But unfortunately for her, the spell she had cast was far from perfect. The fall into the puddle had washed one of the plates, and the spell could only work properly on unused, unwashed plates. Just as she was about to shout something like 'So long, suckers!' and fly away, the spell was broken (I don't think anyone in those days would ever have said 'So long, suckers!' but you get the idea).

She plummeted down into the big pile of firewood, and the people jumped forward and set light to it. Well, I won't dwell on the gory details, but pretty soon she was all burned up. It was a bad end for her, though what happened to the other Wallsend Witches who escaped that night from the Church, I don't know. I've never heard of them being seen again. Of course, that's assuming the story is true at all – after all, witches were not burned in England but hanged, and Lord Delaval who told the story was famous for making up tall tales and outrageous lies. I've been to Wallsend as well, and never seen anyone who looked like a witch. But then, what do I know?

THE
NEWCASTLE
WITCHES

We might not know if the story of the Wallsend Witches is really true or not, but there's no doubt at all about the Newcastle Witches. In 1649 and 1650, Newcastle played host to one of the biggest witch trials in English history! In March 1649 the council of Newcastle received a letter from some concerned citizens – they were worried that the town had been cursed by evil witches, who were even now plotting some even worse evil deeds!

So, they did what they thought was best and sent some of their men into Scotland to fetch the Witchfinder! Witchfinding was a real job back in those days, and most witch hunters were suspicious men in black cloaks and tall black hats. The Witchfinder carried the tool of his trade with him – a long spike that he jabbed people with. If they bled or cried out when his spike stabbed them, then they were declared innocent. But if the spike didn't make them bleed, or they couldn't feel anything when he stabbed them, then they must be witches, and were sentenced to death! He pronounced to anyone who would listen that he was a real artist, and that his art was hunting witches. He charged 20 shillings for every witch that he found, and, all over Scotland, towns had been only too eager to pay him. Now the people of Newcastle got their pennies together and hoped that he could sniff out the witches who were hiding among them.

The town crier went around ringing his bell and shouting that anyone who thought their neighbour or mother-in-law might be a witch should bring them to be tried at the Town Hall. There the Witchfinder set about his business, and people were amazed when many of the people he jabbed with his spike did not bleed and felt no pain! Witches! All those whom the Witchfinder declared guilty were taken to prison to await their execution.

All except one – a young woman who was brought up on trial was saved by a man called Colonel Hobson, a doctor in the army. He saw the Witchfinder fiddling with his spike before

he jabbed her and thought that something odd was going on. Sure enough, when the Witchfinder stabbed her there was no blood, and she didn't seem to feel anything.

'Witch!' everyone began to cry out, but Colonel Hobson stood up.

'Wait!' he cried out. 'She's just embarrassed, so she blushed and all the blood rushed to her cheeks and so she didn't bleed. Let me try.'

He took out a sharp spike from his doctor's bag and jabbed the girl, and sure enough she bled and let out a sharp 'ouch!' and she was saved.

But eighteen others were not so lucky – a few days later seventeen women and one man were hanged on the town moor for the crime of witchcraft, their bodies buried in unmarked graves in St Andrew's Churchyard. The Witchfinder went back to Scotland carrying his money – which would be worth more than £2000 today! But a few months later, news reached Newcastle from Scotland: the Witchfinder had been arrested! When he was examined, they found he had a fake spike that could slip back

into the handle, like the fake knives that they use in plays. He was a fraud! All the people hanged had been innocent, just as Colonel Hobson had suspected – at least he'd been able to save one.

I'm sorry I couldn't give the story a happier ending, but there it is. Or is it? In fact, over 350 years later in 2008 workmen were digging in a forgotten corner of St Andrew's Churchyard, when they dug up a pile of old bones – the bones of the witches! One of the workmen said that where he had touched the bones, he came up in horrible itchy spots and red marks. I guess even after 350 years, people are still pretty quick to attribute any injury or bad luck to witchcraft. So be wary of witch hunts and Witchfinders, my friends – you're probably better off with witches!

SUPER
HERO
SAINT

Cuthbert was a nine-year-old boy playing with his friends among the hills of Melrose in Scotland. They were running this way and that when Cuthbert ran straight into a man wearing long robes.

'Sorry!' Cuthbert called. 'I'm so sorry!'

'It's alright,' the man smiled, 'but why do you play with children … Bishop Cuthbert?'

Then the man disappeared.

Bishop Cuthbert? The boy wondered. What did that mean? Why had the man called him a bishop? A bishop was a very important person!

Years later Cuthbert had taken the job as a shepherd in Northumberland. He was sixteen and needed his sleep. The teenager laid back upon the spiky grass of the coastland hills. The sheep were sleeping. The air was mild. Life was good. He sighed and closed his eyes. He was just nodding off to sleep when he heard a huge choral cry in the distance. He sat up and looked along the coastline. Above a castle on a hill, a cloud was glowing white. Angels were singing loudly as they flew down from above. They seemed to be carrying somebody up from the castle. The angels shone with bright white light, they had six wings each and their halos shone like headlights. The body was taken upwards into the clouds, then they disappeared.

Cuthbert was left in darkness. His wide eyes blinked several times. Angels? Angels! He had seen angels and his life would never be the same again.

How could he be a shepherd now, when he had seen *with his own eyes* real life angels? He decided right there and then that he would become a monk and serve God. He would give his life to serving God. He wanted the angels to come for him when he died, just like the man from the castle.

Cuthbert went to the nearest monastery that night and signed up for the life of a monk. He toured Northumberland with other monks to tell the North East of England about God. It was while he wandered the beautiful landscape that he began to listen. To

really listen. He found that when he listened, he heard things. It was on this tour that he discovered that when he listened, he heard not only people but animals too! Cuthbert had a secret super power. He could understand the language of the animals and they could understand him too!

The birds would chat to him. The fish would say hello. Even the spiders would wave a leg or eight as he passed by. The animals would talk and he would reply. They looked after him too. When he was hungry, the birds brought him food. When he went into the sea to pray, the seals would give him a cuddle to keep him warm.

But it was the Eider ducks that loved Cuthbert most. These sea ducks would keep him company in his home.

'Quack!' That was what others heard.

'Morning!' That was what Cuthbert heard.

Cuthbert had moved to a little island near to a slightly larger island called Lindisfarne. The monks from the monastery on Lindisfarne would visit Cuthbert and ask him questions about God and life itself. Cuthbert would reply with wise words learnt from the animals, all the while surrounded by the creatures he loved so much. But the Eider ducks would always be cuddled up on his knee, the closest of all. They didn't call him Cuthbert, but Cuddy instead, for short.

Monk Cuthbert later became Bishop Cuthbert of Lindisfarne, just as the stranger had predicted many years before. But Bishop Cuthbert became an old man and died. He had been travelling north preaching the Word of God. The animals and the other monks he had been travelling with took him back to Lindisfarne, where he was placed in a coffin and buried in the churchyard. It was the only funeral that has ever been attended by both humans and animals.

Eleven years later, with stories of Cuthbert and the animals being told far and wide, the monastery was visited by many people wanting to see the coffin of this amazing monk. The other monks decided to bring the coffin into the church to make it easier to see. The coffin was dug up and the monks peered inside. Cuthbert looked to be simply sleeping! His body had not changed at all. It was decided that this was a miracle and the monk was made a saint.

Saint Cuthbert! The little boy from Scotland who had become a shepherd and then a monk in the hills of Northumberland. The man who could talk to animals. It was this super hero saint who would later travel to the rivers of Tyne and Wear and change the North East of England forever…

SAINT CUTHBERT'S JOURNEY

The monastery of Lindisfarne was filled with treasure. There was gold and silver. There was even a leather-bound book of gospels decorated with gold and jewels. But the most important treasure was the body of a saint. Saint Cuthbert's body lay proudly in his coffin on Lindisfarne. People travelled for miles to meet the super hero monk, even though he was dead!

The monks who lived in the monastery were happy. But then some most unwelcome visitors arrived. Visitors huge and hairy. Visitors with swords and spears. Visitor Vikings!

They arrived in their long boats from Scandinavia and they arrived to steal treasure. The viking raiders ran towards the monastery and the monks saw them coming. The monks grabbed what they could and ran. They grabbed the book of gospels and the coffin of Cuthbert and were off.

The Vikings stole everything else and were delighted with their hoard. They returned to their ships but would come back to these lands

many times more. They eventually decided not only to raid there but to settle down too.

Meanwhile, the monks travelled with Cuthbert and the book. They tried to cross the sea to reach the monasteries of Ireland, but a great storm rose. The monks were drenched and terrified. They took this to be a sign from God not to cross the sea, so they continued to travel around England. They stopped at Derwent, Whithorn, Crayke and Chester-le-Street, but eventually found themselves wandering the twists and turns of the River Wear.

It was on the banks of the river that the monks got stuck. SLUUUUUUURP! The wheels of their wagon oozed into the thick mud.

'Stop!' called one of the monks. 'You're making it worse!'

'Back it up!' called another.

'It won't budge!'

'What will we do?'

The wagon would not move. The monks tried and tried and tried again, but still it would not move.

'Let us pray!' one of the monks announced. 'God will guide us!'

The monks all nodded in agreement. They knelt on the river bank and closed their eyes. The sound of the fast-running water filled their ears. Birds sang, insects chirped, wind whistled. They waited for an answer.

Finally, it arrived.

'Dunholme!' one of the monks suddenly blurted out, getting to his feet.

The other monks opened their eyes and stared at him.

'Eh?'

'Dunholme!' he said again.

'What's that?'

'It's where we are to take Saint Cuthbert!'

The monks all stood.

'God told me that we are to take the body to Dunholme!' the monk announced, beaming.

The other monks returned the smile.

'Great!' said one. 'Where's that?'

They all looked at the monk who had been spoken to by God. His face fell.

'I don't know,' he sighed. 'God didn't tell me that bit.'

They all groaned and sighed. They looked around for street signs but there were none.

Just then a big, brown cow went walking past. The monks watched its slow, swaying swagger. It went into the forest nearby and was gone.

'So, what do we do now?' asked a monk.

Their attention was distracted once again by a girl running toward them.

'Have you seen a cow?' she called to them.

The monks nodded as one. She stopped in front of them, breathless and panting.

'Great!' she gasped. 'Where?'

The monks pointed toward the forest.

'Right, thanks.' With that the girl raced off into the forest. 'I've got to take it to the market at Dunholme!' she shouted back over her shoulder.

Dunholme! The monks all stared at one another.

'Let's follow that girl!'

'Let's follow that cow!'

'But the wagon's stuck!'

The monks sighed and turned their heads towards the wagon.

'Let's try it again.'

The wheels moved effortlessly through the mud. They quickly followed the girl into the woods. She had caught up with the cow and had tied a thick rope around its neck. The cow turned toward the monks. It slowly stomped towards them and nudged its muzzle against the coffin.

'Can we come with you?' the monks asked the girl. 'Can you take us to Dunholme?'

She smiled back at them and nodded.

The monks followed the girl and the cow through the woods. They saw Dunholme in the distance. They also saw that beyond the market town there was a little hill circled by a glinting river.

'There,' one of the monks sighed. 'Saint Cuthbert's new home.'

All of the monks nodded. It was perfect.

The coffin of Saint Cuthbert was buried on top of the hill and a wooden church was built on top. The super hero saint was finally in his home, in a place we now call Durham.

THE
FLYING
DONKEY

I'm sure people are always keen to tell you about how they used to entertain themselves 'back in their day'.

'We didn't have the internet back in my day,' they'll say, and then go on to tell you about how they used to pass the time by sitting in front of the television with only four channels, or by playing cards or singing songs around the family piano or whatever it was.

But as annoying as that can be, it's true that people have always sought to entertain themselves, often in pretty strange ways. In fact, some of the things that people used to find entertaining can seem downright crazy to us now. A case in point is this story – the story of the Flying Man and his donkey. The oddest thing about this story is that it's totally true – it was reported in the newspapers in Newcastle back in 1733 …

'Have you heard about the Flying Man? They say he's amazing! They say he can soar over the rooftops and shoot down to the ground faster than a bullet from a gun! My mam says he's the most amazing performer she's ever seen, and he only comes to town every few years and we'd better see him while we have the chance! Besides, the rumour is he has something really amazing this year!'

If you'd lived in Newcastle back then, that was the word on the street – everyone was talking about the amazing flying man and the feats he was going to perform. Now, when I say 'flying man' you might be imagining someone with a pair of wings strapped to his back, or someone a bit like Superman. A flying man was actually someone who used a rope to slide down from the tops of high buildings to the ground at amazing speed, astonishing everyone watching. Partly, this was because the stunts the flying men performed were incredibly dangerous! Most flying men didn't have a very long career because eventually a rope would be too loose and the flying man would SPLAT into the ground at high speed; or the rope would be too tight and would snap and the flying man really would fly off into the distance, and then would come CRASHING down to the ground.

People liked entertainment with a sense of danger back then, so flying men were very popular and could make a lot of money. So, on 23 April 1733, a huge crowd gathered at the base of the Castle Keep in Newcastle, straining their eyes to see the tiny figure moving around on the top of the ancient stone tower – the Flying Man, Mr Violante! Then, with a leap he jumped to the top of the ancient wall, flung a leather handle around the rope that ran from the roof to the ground and jumped from the top!

Everyone held their breath as with a WHOOSH he shot from the sky and fell to the ground as fast as a firework. Then he climbed the tower and came down again; and again! Each time he performed the most amazing acrobatic tricks on the rope and the people gasped with amazement and clapped and cheered. Finally, he leapt and slid down the rope head first before leaping off at the last moment and landing with a somersault on his feet! The roars of the crowd were deafening, but then Mr Violante, the Flying Man, held up his hands for quiet. The crowd grew hushed to hear what he would say.

'My friends! You have seen the amazing feats that only I, the legendary Flying Man, can perform! But today you are going to see something that has never been seen before. From the roof of this ancient castle you are about to see a mere beast perform the feats that have astonished you. You've seen the Flying Man, now prepare yourself for ... the Flying Donkey!'

The crowd cheered but many people were confused and mumbled to one another. A flying donkey? They all lifted their heads and peered at the top of the crumbling old castle in front of them – sure enough, there on the top of the walls was a donkey being led by the Flying Man's assistant. Slowly, they attached a kind of harness to the donkey, and tied it to the rope which ran from the top of the castle and into the street below. Then all the people held their breath as with one mighty shove, the donkey went over the edge!

To say that it flew would be an insult to birds – the Flying Donkey plummeted! To help it on its journey to the ground it had weights tied onto its legs, and these caused the donkey's limbs to wave wildly in every direction. It brayed and shouted as it shot towards the ground, and the crowds looked on in horror – unlike the Flying Man, the donkey could not get off the rope!

With a sound that had never been heard before and will hopefully never be heard again, the legendary Flying Donkey of Old Newcastle Town smashed into the crowd. Added to the noise of crashing donkey were the donkey's braying yells, the cries and screams of the crowd and the noise of people falling to the ground as they tried to duck under the donkey when it shot overhead. Finally, it came to a stop as it hit the ground, its fall broken by the many, many people it had crashed into on its

way to earth. When the dust cleared and the people looked around them, the Flying Man was nowhere to be seen. Seeing the disaster he had caused, he'd decided to get out of town as quickly as he could and had run away before anyone had seen him.

All that was left of the disaster were the bruised bodies of the poor people who couldn't get out of the donkey's way, and a rather confused-looking donkey with weights tied to its feet – somehow, by a miracle, it had survived the fall! The strange story was reported in Newcastle's newspapers, but soon had passed into legend. Whenever anyone in Newcastle heard someone boast that a Flying Man had visited their town, they would say, 'Aye, anyone can see a MAN fly. But have ye heard of the Flying Donkey?'

THE
CAULD
LAD OF
HYLTON

The ghost of Hylton Castle was a little boy who was as lonely as a pea rolling around an empty school dinner hall. He wandered up and down the corridors of the castle. He floated up and down the staircases. He drifted through the walls, entering room after room. He sat atop the battlements and stared out at the river in the distance.

During the day, he simply watched the activities of the castle. He peeked round corners, peered from behind curtains and peeped from under beds. But, when they all were asleep on a night, the ghost was simply lonely.

It was this loneliness that led the ghost to mischief. Boredom often does that. During boring lessons at school, it is tempting to start your own fun. That was how the ghost felt.

So, he began to tip salt into the flour, mix the sugar with spices and put pepper into the tea leaves. But still he felt lonely and began to become more destructive. He smashed plates, toppled tables and pulled clothes from their drawers.

The next morning, the servants would have to clean it all up and the ghost sat back and watched. It proved to be great entertainment. The ghost spent the day stifling his laughter as the servants huffed and puffed, putting the castle back in order. His giggles were often heard from the other side of doors, behind curtains and under beds.

The ghost made more mischief besides. He played football with the potatoes in the kitchen, decorated the bathrooms with bras and pants, then wrote rude words on the dining room floor with flour.

'It's getting worse!' the servants moaned.

'What will we do?' they asked.

'Who can help us?'

They had heard of a wise woman who lived down to the south of the Wear. They decided to pay her a visit and ask for help.

After a long journey on an uncomfortable carriage, the servants knocked at the door and waited. Then the door was flung open and there she stood: the wise woman of the Wear.

'Hiya!' she croaked.

'Erm, hello, wise woman,' the servants mumbled nervously. 'We seek your help.'

'Call me Tia!' she grinned, revealing teeth that resembled a mixed-up pile of jigsaw pieces in grey, yellow and black. 'What's up?'

'We have a mischievous ghost at Hylton Castle,' the servants explained. 'He smashes things up every night and causes all kinds of bother.'

'Only at night, you say?' Tia rubbed her hairy, wart-infested chin and made a 'hmmm' sound. Sounds like he's a brownie,' she said at last, 'not the kind full of chocolate either.'

'A what?'

'A brownie,' Tia cackled. 'That's what they do.'

'So, what do *we* do?'

'Nothing!' laughed the wise woman. 'Do nothing and this brownie will clean it all up for you!'

'Really?'

'Yup! But if you want to give the little thing a treat then make him some clothes. He's cold you see, ever so cold. If you make him shoes, a cloak and hat, he'll be happy!'

The servants huddled and whispered to one another animatedly.

'That it?' the wise woman asked.

'Thank you so much, oh wise one!' the servants said, smiling. Then they were off back to the castle. The coach was filled with planning and chatter.

That night, the servants listened as the ghost smashed and bashed around the castle all night long.

In the morning, they sat at the dining room table and sipped their tea amid the destruction all around.

When they went for a stroll around the grounds, the ghost set to work tidying the mess he had made.

'She was right!' the servants said, listening to the sounds from the castle.

They went off to the tailor's in the market and ordered brown leather shoes, a white silk cloak and a fine green hat.

When they arrived back in the castle, they saw it looking more pristine than it had ever looked before.

'I like this!' the chef said. 'Why don't we let him do all of the work in the castle?'

'Hush your nonsense!' the maid replied. 'We won't have a poor, lonely and cold boy do the work for us in this castle!'

'Indeed!' added the butler. 'He's our ghost and we'll see him right.'

The chef nodded.

'I'll light a fire in the kitchen for him. Put the clothes by that to keep them warm.'

The servants didn't go to bed that night. They hid under the kitchen table or in the pantry.

The ghost came floating through the door and stopped when he saw the pile of clothes. The servants could see his cold, blue glow shining in the darkness. The ghost slipped on the shoes, cloak and hat. He jumped for joy and clicked his heels together.

'Here's a cloak and here's a hood! The Cauld Lad of Hylton will do no more good!'

His glow shifted from blue to orange and he smiled the broadest smile any of the servants had ever seen before or since. Then the ghost floated off in his new clothes and was never seen again. But sometimes, if you listen very carefully, you can hear the ghost's giggle in the castle.

HALF-HANGED MACDONALD

wan MacDonald was the apple of his mother's eye – that is to say, she loved him very much. She cried a bit when she sent him off to join the army, but join he did. He marched off from the Highlands of Scotland where he was born and down south to England.

This was back in the days after 1745 when a great Scottish army had marched down into England and back again and had been beaten only after hard fighting. In revenge the government in England had banned the wearing of kilts, the playing of bagpipes and anything else that reminded them of the fierce Highlanders who had fought against them. The only exception was for those who joined the British Army – the regiments of Highlanders marched into battle in their tartan kilts to the sound of the wailing of bagpipes and were known everywhere they went as brave and fierce warriors with fierce tempers to match.

Ewan MacDonald was no exception to the rule. Even though he had just turned seventeen years old, he was almost seven feet tall in his bare feet, with a shock of bright red hair and the beginnings of a beard. His arms and legs were as thick as tree trunks – you or I would certainly not pick a fight with him! This young giant marched off in full Highland dress, with his kilt wrapped around his body, a dagger tucked into his long socks and carrying his long musket.

After several days of marching, General Guise's new regiment of Highland soldiers came to the River Tyne and the town where they were to make their base for the next few weeks – Newcastle. As they marched into the town, past the ruins of the old town walls which had been built in medieval times to keep out Scottish raiders, we can only imagine what the crowds of people who gathered to watch and stare at them must have thought.

It was only a few years since these fierce Highlanders had invaded England, and Newcastle had been fortified against them. Not only that, but the people of Newcastle had fought against the Scots for hundreds of years before England and Scotland were united as one country – it was still thought to be a terrible insult to call someone a 'Scots rogue', and Scottish people were not allowed to settle or work in the town or open their own shops. To the people of Newcastle, these Highlanders were rough barbarians who couldn't speak English. To the Highlanders, the people of Newcastle were soft southerners who lived in a cramped and stinking town. To say they didn't like each other would be an understatement!

So, it should come as no surprise that there was trouble in the town while the Highland regiment was staying. This is how it happened.

Ewan MacDonald and his friends had been let out of their barracks to go and enjoy themselves in the town of Newcastle, and like many soldiers before them and many after, they had gone to the pubs to drink beer and dance and enjoy themselves. Ewan and the Highlanders were drinking in one of the many pubs in the street called the Bigg Market – perhaps in the

Flying Horse, which we will hear more about later on! Maybe they had a little bit too much beer to drink, and maybe not. What I do know is that when the locals starting to laugh at them for wearing skirts (which is what their kilts looked like to the eyes of the people of Newcastle) they got angry; VERY angry.

Shouted words became flying fists and soon the whole of Bigg Market was in an uproar. People were thrown through the windows of the pubs into the street, and then came striding back in through the doors. In the middle of it all was Ewan MacDonald, who had been especially picked upon because of his size. Though he was big he was normally a gentle young man, but he was so angry that he fought with all his strength. He broke the arm of one bully, and the leg of another. All of this might have been overlooked, but when a whole gang of people grabbed hold of him, Ewan grabbed for the dagger in his sock. Afterwards he said he didn't remember doing it – that the dagger just seemed to be there in his hand.

But when the sun rose the next day, one of the bullies from Newcastle lay dead in the street with Ewan MacDonald's dagger in his heart. Ewan was arrested and taken to the courthouse where he pleaded with the judge, saying that he had never meant to hurt the man and had only been trying to defend himself against a whole gang of people.

The judge did not listen to the young Highlander, and when the trial was over, the judge put on his black hat and told everyone assembled for the trial the sentence that would be passed for murder: Ewan MacDonald would be taken from prison to the Town Moor, and then hanged until he was dead. And that wasn't the worst of it! Once he was dead his body would be given to the surgeons, to be chopped up so they could learn more about how the human body worked. In those days, many people were very afraid of doctors or surgeons because they were always looking for bodies to chop up as practice, and they couldn't get very many except when murderers were hanged.

Now, I apologise if this gruesome little story has scared you, but it doesn't get any less gruesome from here! Ewan MacDonald was taken to the Town Moor just as the judge had said. The people of Newcastle lined the way and went to watch – truth be told, they felt very bad for the young man. He had after all been bullied and provoked, and they didn't really think he was a bad person. But the law didn't much care if he was nice or nasty. He was taken and hanged until he was dead. His body was cut down and taken to the Guild of Surgeons.

The building is still there now, standing just opposite the Laing Art Gallery in the centre of Newcastle, and I've often thought it was a pretty spooky place. The people of Newcastle in those days must have thought so too, and they told awful stories about what the surgeons got up to in there. But the truth is that they were honest doctors, and they needed to cut open the bodies of dead people to get an idea of how living bodies worked, so that they would be able to save people who were sick or wounded.

Three of these surgeons and one apprentice gathered around a long table where lay the dead body of poor Ewan MacDonald. The surgeons would cut up the body while the student would take notes – or at least, that was the plan. Just as they were about to begin, the door to the room burst open and a man ran in, shouting that the mayor had taken ill and was calling for doctors and surgeons! The three surgeons rushed out and left the dissection in the hands of their apprentice.

He was nervous – of course, alone in a cold room lit only by candles with the dead body of a murderer, who wouldn't be? But he was also excited – this was his chance to practise all the things he had been learning about. He reached down with a long, sharp knife, but just as it touched Ewan MacDonald, the young surgeon screamed out loud! Ewan MacDonald screamed too and sat bolt upright on the table! He hadn't been hanged to death at all – he was only half dead, or half-hanged, you might say. Now if you're expecting me to give you

a happy ending where Ewan comes back to life and the judge decides to let him off from being hanged a second time, I'm afraid that I'm going to disappoint you.

The terrified surgeon's apprentice grabbed for the wooden mallet lying on the table nearby and with a desperate swing of his arm cracked poor old Ewan MacDonald over the head. He fell back onto the table – this time he really was dead. At first, the young apprentice surgeon felt a little guilty, but he soon realised that everything was as it should be, and by the time the more experienced surgeons had come back from attending the mayor, the young man was cleaning up the mess.

Of course, when the story got out (as stories always do), the people of the town were not happy – it just confirmed that the surgeons were a scary bunch who were up to no good. No one was surprised when the young apprentice surgeon was found dead in his stable one day; some people said that some of Ewan's friends in the Highland regiment came to get their own back on him; some said that he was just kicked by his horse; but some said that the ghost of Half-Hanged MacDonald came and found his killer and frightened him to death! Who am I to say otherwise?

THE
EVIL
FAIRIES
OF
STANHOPE

Kimberley Wimberley ran down to the River Wear. She was skimming stones when she saw them. They were about the size of a bottle of milk and they were dancing. Some played instruments, others were singing, some were hovering above the ground on wings. But they all moved to the music. They were fairies! Real-life, actual fairies.

Kimberley gasped. She crouched low to the floor as she looked on. The fairies gathered in a large circle and began to spin. They turned and turned and turned. The girl was mesmerised.

Then the little flying creatures did a dance where they clapped hands and knocked knees. Kimberley loved the sight so much that she let out a little giggle.

Then the fairies stopped.

They turned as one to face her. Their little eyes narrowed. Kimberley was terrified. She jumped up and ran home as fast as she could.

'Dad!' she called, bursting through the door. 'Dad! I saw fairies down by the river!'

Winston Wimberley jumped to his feet.

'Fairies, you say?' His face was full of worry.

'Is that bad?' the girl asked.

He nodded gravely in reply and grabbed her hand. 'We need to seek out Tia Maria!'

'Who?'

'You'll see,' Winston replied, and then they were off.

They travelled on a chestnut horse as swift as the wind, following the river as their guide. Eventually, they arrived at a tumble-down cottage and knocked at the door.

Kimberley bit back her surprise when the woman opened the door. Her teeth sank down onto her lower lip as she took in the scene. Tia Maria had shaved recently but her stubble was still thick and dark. She had trimmed her nasal hair but had forgotten about the hair that hung long and loose from her ears.

'Hiya!' she croaked.

'Hello, oh wise woman,' Winston replied.

'What's up?'

Winston nudged Kimberley.

'I saw fairies,' the girl said softly.

Tia Maria shook her head slowly. Her ear lobes wobbled like pendulous baubles.

'That's not good,' she rasped.

Kimberley looked up at her Dad.

'But there is a solution!'

'Hoorah!' Kimberley cried and clapped her hands.

'The fairies will come for you tonight, Kimberley Wimberley,' the old woman said slowly,. 'They will come but if there is no sound from your house at all then they will leave you alone!'

'Got it,' nodded Kimberley.

'Got it,' added Winston. 'Thank you so much, oh wise one.'

The pair turned and climbed onto the horse. They waved to the wise woman as they raced away.

'Not a sound!' Tia Maria called after them.

They arrived back at their home and stopped to listen. They heard the crackle from the fire, the ticking of the clock and the dripping of the tap. The fire was put out, the clock stopped and the tap fixed. They listened again and not a sound could be heard.

After an evening meal of sausages and beans the pair went to their rooms and stayed as quiet and still as a mouse in a cattery. But soon Winston felt the familiar rumble in his passageways. What on earth had made him make beans for tea? Beans!

As darkness descended over the house, there was something descending in Winston. He held his buttocks tightly. He concentrated so hard on making the wind go back up, but in the end it was no use.

THHHHHWWWWWWWPPPPPP PPPPTTTTTTTTTT!

The furious gust squeaked out of him. Then the door burst open and the fairies flew up the stairs.

Winston raced to his daughter's room but Kimberley was gone.

'Nooooo!' he cried.

He was out of the door, on his horse and racing towards Tia Maria's house faster than a cheetah with a jet pack. He hammered at the door.

Tia Maria opened the door in her nightie. The description of her has been removed from this book so as not to disturb younger readers, older readers and the dead.

'She's been taken!' Winston blurted out.

'Beans?' the old woman asked.

He nodded, red faced.

'It's always the beans that does it,' she said, shaking her head. 'Don't worry, Winston. There's something you can do.'

'What?' he gasped desperately.

'First, you need a light that does not burn. Second, a chicken with no bones in its body. Third, a part of an animal that has not lost a drop of blood. Take those three things to the cave of the fairies down at the source of the River Wear. By fairy law, they will have to give her back to you.'

'Thanks!'

Winston was back on the horse and galloping towards Wearhead near to his Stanhope home. His mind was racing. How on earth would he get those three things? The light, the chicken and the animal part? It was crazy!

He was riding so fast that he almost didn't see the soft light glowing from the muddy track. He brought his horse screeching to a halt, slid down from the saddle and ran back toward it. There were several lights in the mud. He pulled one free and saw it was a glow-worm.

'A light that does not burn!' he cried, delightedly.

He hopped back in the saddle and rode off down the track with the glow-worm safely in his pocket.

Then he noticed a farmhouse, with a sign selling eggs. He had an idea and knocked at the door.

'Who's there, banging at my door in the middle of the night?' barked a voice from inside.

'Sorry to disturb you but I need an egg!' Winston replied.

The farmer flung open the door with an angry expression upon his face. Winston held out a gold coin.

The farmer's face flashed brightly.

'Any particular kind of egg, sir?' the farmer beamed.

'I need one that holds a baby chick yet unborn, but so new the chick has no bones in its body!'

The farmer looked a little confused at first but then ran off to the hen house and came back holding the exact egg that Winston needed.

'Thanks!'

Winston was off again with the egg in one pocket and the glow-worm in the other. But where to find a part of an animal that hasn't lost a drop of blood? He pondered this the whole speedy ride to the source of the river. Then he saw it.

The cave sat small and dark like a black beady eye. He knew straight away that it had to be the home of the fairies. He tethered his horse and walked slowly forward. A silver moon hung in the sky, lighting his way. It was then he noticed several newts climbing out of the river on their nightly hunt for slugs and worms.

Winston grabbed one by its tail. It slithered and slimed and tried to crawl away. When Winston would not let go, the newt pushed itself so hard that its tail came off in the man's hand. Not a drop of blood came from it.

He had the three things!

He stepped towards the cave. Then he put down the worm, egg and tail, and waited. Tiny hands reached out and grabbed the three things. Only a few seconds passed, but to Winston it seemed like years. Then, suddenly, the cave entrance widened like a yawning mouth. Kimberley climbed up and out. She was free! Winston grabbed her by the hand and the pair raced to the horse.

'You rescued me!'

Kimberley and Winston raced home. They did not have beans for dinner for quite some time after that!

BRANCEPETH'S BRAWN

Roger de Ferry was a knight from Ferryhill. He was brave, he was handsome, he was clever – but he had a problem. A piggy problem. A very large piggy problem. There was a giant boar known as a 'brawn' which had been attacking the people who lived around Ferryhill. This was no ordinary pig. It had long tusk teeth that were like the horns of the Minotaur. The bristles on its skin were thick as knives and just as sharp. It had developed a taste for human flesh and had been gobbling up anyone it could find.

'A killer pig?!' Roger had gasped at the very idea.

The three servants at his home in Brancepeth Castle had told him all about it when he returned home from battles far away.

'But really?' he asked. 'A human-eating, killer pig?'

The servants explained that knights from all around Tyne and Wear had come to defeat the pig but all had failed.

'Yeah, but I mean really? A gigantic, human-eating, killer pig?'

The servants begged Roger not to go, for he would surely die.

'I shall face this gigantic, human-eating, killer pig and I shall slay the beast myself!'

He stood heroically as he said this, but he had to admit that it did sound scary.

With his horse groomed, armour polished and sword sharpened he was ready for the epic battle to commence. He had fought many battles and won every one. Surely a pig would not beat him. Even a gigantic, human-eating, killer pig!

Roger galloped away from the castle and along to a crossroads at Cleves Cross. He would charge back and forth on his horse and hack the thing into pork chops! His horse stamped nervously upon the path as they waited. Thick clouds of steam snorted from its nostrils.

Then, Roger saw it. It was very hard not to see it, as the pig was roughly the size of a small planet. His servants had not been exaggerating. In fact, if anything, they had understated the

beast's size, deadliness and ferocity. The eyes glowed a manic red, the trotters bore massive bladed toenails.

Roger gulped. His horse looked on wide eyed and even wider mouthed.

'Get ready, Hercules,' Roger whispered into his horse's ear. 'We're going in!'

The pig seemed to have only just spotted Roger on his horse. It roared with rage at someone daring to stand on its path. The roar sounded like an orchestra of a thousand dragons.

Hercules the horse began to tremble. Or perhaps it was Roger who was shaking so much that his horse was wobbling beneath him.

The boar continued its roar and charged at the pair. Hercules turned and ran as fast as his four hooves would carry him. So, it was the horse that had been shaking. They could hear the roar getting quieter as the two raced over the land and back to the safety of the castle.

'How did you get on?' one of the servants asked.

'Did you kill it?' another put in.

'Is it pork chops for tea?'

Roger jumped down from the saddle.

'I'm afraid not,' he sighed. 'I think we need a rather different approach to this.'

Hercules was nodding his long head in agreement as he was taken off to the stables. Roger went off to his room to spend the night thinking.

Morning arrived and Roger was ready. He hadn't slept a minute and was exhausted, but at least he had a plan!

'Should I ready your horse?' a servant asked.

Roger shook his head.

'Polish your armour?'

More head shaking.

'Sharpen your sword?'

A bit more shaking.

'I need a very long spear and a spade!'

The servants scurried off to get the two things. Roger then went to see Hercules in the stables.

'Right, old friend,' he said to his horse, 'there's good news and bad news. Which first?'

The horse stamped his foot.

'Bad news it is! I'm afraid we have to go back to meet that pig.'

Hercules' eyes widened in terror. He snorted loudly.

'Good news?' Roger laughed nervously. 'Well, I need a lift there and then you can come straight back here.'

Hercules neighed loudly and nodded.

'Let's go then, old friend!'

Roger collected the spear and spade, then was off on Hercules, racing at speed back to Cleves Cross.

Once down from the saddle, Roger patted a fond farewell and Hercules was out of there quicker than a rocket full of monkeys. The knight sighed as he watched the horse go.

Then Roger got to work, digging a vast hole. It took him all day but he did it. He'd dug a hole to trap the pig and used the extra-long spear to help him climb out. The hole was then covered with branches, leaves and twigs.

Hiding in some bushes, the knight waited. He didn't wait long before the ground began to shake and the gigantic, human-eating, killer pig came thundering along the path. Roger bounced up and down, up and down as each heavy trotter thudded towards him. He peered out and saw the pig's snout, sniffing and snorting as it went. Thick, yellow snot dripped rhythmically as it got nearer and nearer. The knight gulped and held his spear even more tightly.

Then the pig stopped. It had stopped right next to the trap. It sniffed the ground. Roger began to shake again. Had it rumbled his trick? Was the pig clever as well as deadly? As if in answer to his questions, the pig stepped forward and fell into the hole with a deafening thud. No, thankfully it wasn't clever.

Roger wasted no time. He burst out of the undergrowth with his spear at the ready. The pig roared and raged in the hole. So, Roger plunged the spear down and the pig was dead!

The knight began to do a little victory dance, but then realised he was being watched. Hercules had brought the servants from the castle.

'You did it!' they chorused.

'I did, didn't I?' laughed Roger. 'Inform the people of Ferryhill that the pig is no more!'

One servant nodded and ran off.

'Look at all this pork! Find a butcher and a chef. We shall all dine on pork chops tonight!'

Another servant ran off.

'Finally, I wonder if we might turn this hole into Ferryhill's first swimming pool!'

The last servant went to run off but didn't know where to go, so just ran around in circles for a bit. Hercules gave Roger a fist bump with his hoof and the pair began to plan a party.

THE HEDLEY KOW

own near the village of Hedley on the Hill, just south of the River Tyne, lived a Kow. Not a cow, mind you – a Kow. There's a difference. A cow has a leg at every corner and gives milk. A Kow – well, that's a different thing entirely. To my knowledge, only the village of Hedley on the Hill ever had a Kow, so it was one of a kind. The Hedley Kow was a type of shapeshifting fairy or goblin – no one knew what it really looked like, because it could change into anything it wanted to, and used to play tricks on the unwary farmers and travellers who passed by Hedley on the Hill.

Often a farmer saw an unattended and fine-looking horse standing in a field and thought to himself, 'Now there's a thing, I've got meself a free horse!' and would throw a rope round its neck to lead it home, only to have the horse (which was really the Kow in disguise) go wild, kicking and neighing and dragging him all around the fields and hills and woodlands all about before dumping him down into a stream or a muddy puddle. Many were the young men

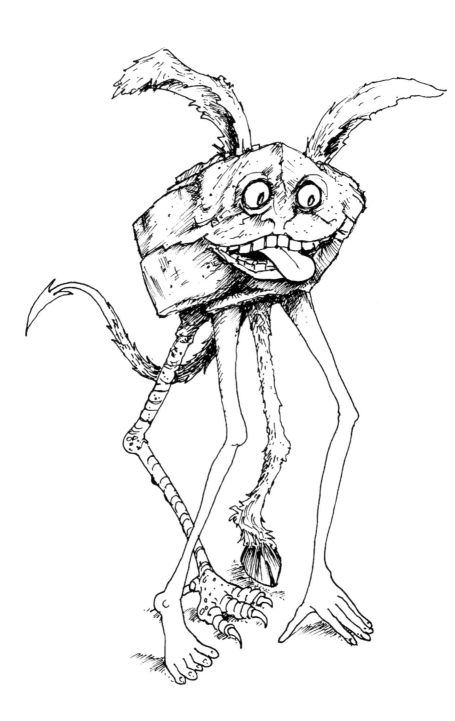

who would go off to meet their girlfriends by a bonny lane at night, and would see their sweethearts walking ahead of them and hear them calling to them. But when they followed them, their friends would lead them off into a tangle of thornbushes or a nasty swamp by the riverside and leave them there – for of course, it wasn't their girlfriend or boyfriend at all, but the Hedley Kow. In the whole village there was hardly a night went by without a milk pail being turned over, plates being smashed, knitting being unravelled, hair being tangled and all kinds of mischief. I suppose a Kow must do something to pass the time, and while it was always annoying the Kow never really hurt anyone or seemed to play any really nasty tricks. It was always the grumpy or greedy who got the worst of it.

Now, it happened that once upon a time in Hedley on the Hill there lived a woman, and she was so poor that it was rare that she had two copper pennies to rub together. She lived by doing odd jobs for people around the village, going from house to house helping out with chores and running errands and carrying messages. She didn't get paid much for it, but people would give her a plate of food in this house, and a cup of tea in the next one, so that she was well enough fed and she always had a cheerful smile on her face – indeed, she often looked much happier than people who had much more than she ever did.

Now, one summer evening she was wandering down the village road back towards her little house and whistling a tune to herself, enjoying the warm air and gazing up at the stars, when she stubbed her toe. She looked down at the road.

'Well, bless me soul if it isn't a big old iron pot! That would be the perfect thing for me to cook my tea in. But who would leave it lying around here?' She looked around in every direction, but she saw no sign of whoever had left the pot.

'Maybe someone has thrown it out. It probably has a big hole in the bottom. Still, it'll be good as a flower pot. I'll just take a look inside …' So she lifted the lid, and she gasped. Inside, the pot was full to the brim with shining gold coins!

'Well, this is amazing! I'm rich! Beyond me wildest dreams. That'll be lovely. I'll just take this home and bury it next to me fireplace and I can go back for some money whenever I need it. Why, I could buy a nice house with this and I'll never have to do a bit of work again!'

She began to drag the pot of gold home, and mighty heavy it was, especially as the night was warm, and soon she was fair dripping with sweat. Eventually she grew tired, and sat down on a hump of grass and decided to rest and check her treasure. But when she looked inside the pot, the gold was gone! Instead of gold coins, there was a big lump of polished silver!

'Well, I could have sworn it was gold coins in there, but this is much better! It'll be much easier to look after a lump of silver than a bunch of gold coins. It would have been a right bother keeping them safe, what with the

burglars and the tax man around. After all, I'm as rich as rich with my lump here!'

And on her way she went until she got tired again, and she sat down, thinking of all the things she would do with her new-found wealth. But when she looked in the pot …

'What's this? I thought it was a lump of silver, but now it's just a big old lump of iron! Well, isn't that amazing – I can sell that very easily, and get a lot of pennies for it as well. Much better than gold or silver – I'd always have been worried about the neighbours finding out and someone robbing me or telling the tax man on me. Yes, this is much better.'

So she started down the hill to her own front door, very pleased with her find – a pot AND a lump of iron! But when she turned round again to check it was still there, there was the pot but inside it was just a big round stone.

'Well, it sure looked like iron before, but I guess it's just a stone. What a lucky find – a pot to cook my dinner in and a nice big stone I can use to hold my door open.'

So she took the stone and stuck it down in front of her door and felt very pleased with herself. A big smile spread across her face when, just then, the stone seemed to laugh! All of a sudden it jumped up into the air and seemed to shake and wobble about with laughter. Four big, long, lanky legs popped out of the stone, then two long ears and a tail, and a face with an absolutely HUGE grin and a pair of big round eyes. With that, the Hedley Kow went trotting off over the hills, shaking its tail and laughing.

'Well I never,' said the woman. 'Aren't I just the luckiest soul in these parts? To see the Hedley Kow all by meself and have such a story to tell about it!'

She went inside to sit by the fire and think on her good luck. And what luck she had – I paid her a penny for that story, and here it is.

THE
LAMBTON
WORM

Young John Lambton was a naughty boy. He never listened to anyone. Not his teachers, not his family, not even his friends. He just spent all of his time running around like a nutter. His parents were the lord and lady of this land. The land that was named after his family. He was young, he was rich and he was very spoilt!

One Sunday, his parents had wanted him to go to church. But John Lambton instead had run off down to the River Wear.

He ran around chasing bees and butterflies, but eventually settled down to do a spot of fishing. He cast his line into the water and sat back. But the rod began to shiver and shake. John expected to find a fat fish on the end of his line, but when he reeled it in there was nothing. So, the boy cast the line again and sat back. As soon as he did, the rod twitched and wobbled. John reeled the line in and again there was nothing. He cast the line for a third time, and as soon as the hook hit the water, the rod shook violently. John angrily reeled the line in again but, the same as before, nothing.

He stood up, shook his fist at the sky and said a lot of rude words. He cursed the river, the land, the people in church, the whole lot. Then he cast the line grumpily into the water once more. The rod buzzed in his hands. But when he reeled in this time, John saw something on the hook. An ugly, evil-looking worm oozed, slithered and slimed all across it.

'Urgh!' John said aloud.

He ripped the worm from the hook and threw it into a well nearby. Then he wiped his hands upon his trousers. He shuddered at the thought of the thing.

He had lost his patience with fishing, so headed back to the castle that was his home. He would have the servants bring him some delicious pies to cheer him up. But what awaited John at the castle was not pies, but rather some news. Some very alarming news.

'It's all been arranged,' Lord Lambton said. 'The final arrangements were organised at church this morning.'

'You should have been there,' Lady Lambton added.

'So, I'm being sent away?!' John asked incredulously. 'Away where?!'

'First you will be a page, then a squire and finally a knight,' his father replied.

'My knight in shining armour!' his mother cooed.

So, John was sent off to train. He would learn to fight and dance and write poetry. All the things knights had to do!

Meanwhile, that worm down the well grew bigger and bigger. It slithered and oozed its way out of the well and saw a duck. It gobbled it up in three bites. Then the worm grew bigger still. It found a chicken, ate that and grew. Found a sheep, ate that and grew. Found a pig, ate that and grew. Found a cow, ate that and was enormous! But the worm then found a taste for human flesh. It ate a farmer and his wife. It ate a whole family out for a walk.

The people of Lambton looked to the lord and lady of the land and asked what should be done. Lord and Lady Lambton gathered all of the knights in their land and sent them to find the dreaded worm. The worm had now grown so large that it could wrap itself around a nearby hill seven times.

The knights knew where to go. It was now named Worm Hill. The hooves thundered and clattered as the horses zoomed to the hill. The knights waved their swords and shouted things like, 'Hazaar!' and 'Woo!' and 'Yay!'

The worm heard them coming. It uncoiled itself and reared up to roar. The knights chopped with their swords and the worm was cut into several pieces.

'Well done chaps!'

The knights all congratulated each other. But while they knuckle bumped and high fived one another, they did not notice the worm joining itself back together.

Sluuuuuuuurp!

The worm then reared up and roared again. So, the knights hacked and chopped, this time making sure the worm was in twice as many pieces.

Sluuuuuuuurp!

The worm was back together. There was more chopping, stabbing, hacking, sawing and cutting.

Sluuuuuuuurp!

It was back. Chop! Chop! Chop!

Sluuuuuuuurp!

Sluuuuuuuurp!

Sluuuuuuuurp!

It was back.

The worm then devoured every last knight and burped loudly at the end.

'I like knights!' it grinned evilly. 'They're crunchy!'

The people of Lambton were distraught. What would they do now?

Lord and Lady Lambton decided that this creature was invincible. The only answer was to feed the worm and keep it happy. So, each day nine cows were tied to a fence near to Worm Hill for the worm to eat. Plus, a huge bath tub was filled with milk for the worm to drink. The worm was happy with this arrangement. But the people of Lambton became poor and starving. Everything they had was sold to pay for worm food.

Years passed. Eventually, John Lambton returned home. He was now a knight! When his parents told him about the worm, he was shocked.

'This is my fault!' he declared. 'I'm the one who fished the worm out of the river when I was young and a nutter. I will deal with it now that I'm a knight!'

He stood heroically for a few moments and then was off.

'He's my knight in shining armour!' his mother gasped.

'He's going to die!' his father declared.

John raced off, not to Worm Hill, but rather to the house of a wise old woman who lived on the other side of the county. He would go and see Tia Maria!

He galloped from Lambton over the hills and far away. It took him a day to follow the path of the River Wear, but at last he made it to her home. He banged at the door with a gauntleted fist.

'Hiya!' she croaked as she opened the door. 'What's up?'

John attempted to ignore the hair that hung from her nostrils and told her the whole tale.

'Ooooh,' sighed Tia Maria. 'Evil worms from rivers are not good. You'll have to do something in return for my help, I'm afraid.'

'Name it!'

'You'll have to kill the first living thing that you meet after the worm is dead.'

'No problem!' he smiled. 'But how do I kill the worm?'

'Don't fight it on dry land,' Tia Maria warned. 'Stand on a rock in the middle of the river.'

'Got it. Anything else?'

'Cover your armour with spikes. If you do those two things then you'll be able to kill the worm.'

John thanked her and sped back to the land of Lambton.

'Don't forget to kill the first living thing that you meet after the worm is dead!' she called after him.

John went home. He told his mother and father what the wise woman had said.

His mother took him to the blacksmith to have his armour covered in spikes. His father took him to the music shop for a trumpet.

'Erm, why would I want a trumpet?' John asked.

'Blow the trumpet, after you kill the worm,' his father replied. 'I'll release a dog from the castle. That will be the first living thing that you meet.'

'Got it!'

John Lambton took his trumpet and his sword. He wore his spiked armour as he strode to the River Wear. He found a flat rock and stood on it. He then began shouting rude things about the worm that slept on Worm Hill beyond. The worm opened its eyes and growled. It uncoiled itself and slithered towards the river.

John held the sword steady and waited. The worm lunged at him. He ducked and sliced off the worm's tail. It plopped into the water and was whisked away by the fast-moving river current.

The worm lunged again and John chopped off more bits.

The worm realised it had been tricked. It wrapped itself around the knight and tried to squeeze him to death. But the spikes chopped it into a hundred pieces and it plopped into the river … dead! John leapt onto the river bank and blew the trumpet.

When his father heard the noise, he was so happy that his son had survived that he raced to the river to meet his son. The first living thing that John saw was his very own Dad. He couldn't bring himself to kill his own father, so they sneaked back to the castle without killing anything else.

Tia Maria had warned them, though. Magic has its own rules. John Lambton had saved the land but a curse was put upon his family. A curse that still remains to this day!

What happened to the Lambtons lives on,
not only in this story, but also in a crazy song …
'Whisht! Lads, haad yer gobs,
An Aa'll tell ye's aall an aaful story
Whisht! Lads, haad yer gobs,
An' Aa'll tell ye 'boot the worm.'

BIBLIOGRAPHY

Brockie, W., *Legends and Superstitions of the County of Durham* (Williams 1886)

Grice, F., *Folk Tales of the North Country* (Thomas Nelson and Sons Ltd 1944)

Hersom, K., *Johnny Reed's Cat and other Northern Tales* (A & C Black 1987)

Hone, W., *The Table Book* (Hunt and Clarke 1827)

Jacobs, J., *More English Fairy Tales* (John D. Batten 1894)

Morgan, J., *Tales of Old Northumberland* (Countryside Books 2006)

Reader's Digest Folklore, Myths and Legends of Britain (Reader's Digest 1977)

Westwood, J. and Simpson J., *The Lore of the Land: A Guide to England's Legends* (Penguin Reference 2005)

The destination for history
www.thehistorypress.co.uk

Society *for* Storytelling

Since 1993, the Society for Storytelling has championed the art of oral storytelling and the benefits it can provide – such as improving memory more than rote learning, promoting healing by stimulating the release of neuropeptides, or simply great entertainment! Storytellers, enthusiasts and academics support and are supported by this registered charity to ensure the art is nurtured and developed throughout the UK.

Many activities of the Society are available to all, such as locating storytellers on the Society website, taking part in our annual National Storytelling Week at the start of every February, purchasing our quarterly magazine *Storylines*, or attending our Annual Gathering – a chance to revel in engaging performances, inspiring workshops, and the company of like-minded people.

You can also become a member of the Society to support the work we do. In return, you receive free access to *Storylines*, discounted tickets to the Annual Gathering and other story-telling events, the opportunity to join our mentorship scheme for new storytellers, and more. Among our great deals for members is a 30% discount off titles in the *Folk Tales* series from The History Press website.

For more information, including how to join, please visit

www.sfs.org.uk